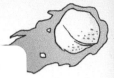

LEO
DA VINCI
vs THE ICE-CREAM DOMINATION LEAGUE

ALSO BY MICHAEL PRYOR

10 Futures

Machine Wars

The EXTRAORDINAIRES series

Book One: The Extinction Gambit

Book Two: The Subterranean Stratagem

The LAWS OF MAGIC series

Book One: Blaze of Glory

Book Two: Heart of Gold

Book Three: Word of Honour

Book Four: Time of Trial

Book Five: Moment of Truth

Book Six: Hour of Need

The CHRONICLES OF KRANGOR series

Book One: The Lost Castle

Book Two: The Missing Kin

Book Three: The King in Reserve

For more information about Michael and his books,
please visit www.michaelpryor.com.au

LEO DA VINCI

vs THE ICE-CREAM DOMINATION LEAGUE

MICHAEL PRYOR

ILLUSTRATED BY JULES FABER

RANDOM HOUSE AUSTRALIA

A Random House book
Published by Random House Australia Pty Ltd
Level 3, 100 Pacific Highway, North Sydney NSW 2060
www.randomhouse.com.au

Penguin
Random House
Australia

First published by Random House Australia in 2015

Random House Books is part of the Penguin Random House group of companies
whose addresses can be found at global.penguinrandomhouse.com.

National Library of Australia
Cataloguing-in-Publication Entry

Author: Pryor, Michael
Title: Leo da Vinci versus the Ice-cream Domination League/Michael Pryor;
illustrated by Jules Faber
ISBN: 978 0 85798 837 9 (pbk)
Series: Pryor, Michael. Leo da Vinci; 1
Target audience: For primary school age
Subjects: Leonardo da Vinci, 1452–1519 – Fiction.
          Adventure stories.
          Friendship – Juvenile fiction.
Other authors/contributors: Faber, Jules
Dewey number: A823.3

Cover and internal illustrations by Jules Faber
Cover design by Rachel Lawston, Lawston Design
Internal design by Midland Typesetters
Printed in Australia by Griffin Press, an accredited ISO AS/NZS 14001:2004
Environmental Management System printer

Random House Australia uses papers that are natural, renewable and recyclable
products and made from wood grown in sustainable forests. The logging and
manufacturing processes are expected to conform to the environmental regulations
of the country of origin.

For all the very fine people from Booked Out —
Lauris, Esther, Simon, Jamie, Emily, Rebecca,
Jen, Tess, Bec, Tanya, Lucy, Alex, Rosalind,
Jack, Lidija, Lauren, Leanne, Hannah,
Danica, Emma and Line.
Many thanks.

CHAPTER 1

Leonardo da Vinci, ten-year-old eagle-eyed righter of wrongs, ate his breakfast with one hand. With his other hand, he sketched a HeliSlide, his latest big idea.

His mother lobbed a banana at him to get his attention. 'Leonardo, someone left a message for you.'

Leo stared at the banana. It gave him an idea for a new kind of skateboard. 'Who was it?'

His mother looked up from her phone. 'He said he was Wild Wilbur, the Destroyer of Worlds. He wanted you to know that he'd broken out of prison and was coming after you. More toast, dear?'

'Yes, please.'

Leonardo da Vinci, genius inventor and Head of Fixit International Inc., frowned. Wild Wilbur was his sixth deadliest enemy. Leo had thought he was rid of him forever after their battle in the Wild Wilbur Black Fortress of Darkest Doom.

Leo added a bubblegum dispenser to the sketch. Wild Wilbur might be wild, but he was also reliable – so Leo had better be alert.

Leo finished his toast. He finished his orange juice. He took his sketch, turned it upside down and wrote his name on it back to front.

'I'm going to the shed,' he said to his mother.

'Make sure you wear a hat,' she replied. 'It's going to be hot again today.'

'Sure.'

'What should I say if Wild Wilbur rings again?'

'Tell him to call my mobile, please.'

Leo zoomed across the backyard and into the shed. He had to jiggle his key in the lock, but eventually he was able to step inside. He made sure to secure the door behind him. This was important. The headquarters of International Fixit Inc. was chock-full of top-secret stuff.

Since Fixit International Inc. was dedi-cated to fixing up anything that needed fixing, Leo collected all sorts of useful bits and pieces, just in case. Lots of boxes, wires, old bottles and crates were stacked up against the walls. Racks of pipes and wires hung from the ceiling. Stairs and lifts led to the seven super-secret underground basements that housed heavy machinery.

What Leo faced when he came in, though, was mostly plans and sketches. Plans and sketches were nailed to walls. Plans and sketches were heaped up on top of other plans and sketches. Leo had to wade through old plans and sketches that had fallen off tall stacks on benches.

'Wild Wilbur is on the loose!' he cried as he pushed aside a mound of sketches for a

Good
Stuff

solar-powered armoured car. He reached a heap of bolts, wires and metal plates.

The pile of junk jerked and clanked. 'No time to worry about that,' it said in a rusty voice. 'Another ice-cream truck has gone missing.'

'What?'

'It's the twenty-sixth ice-cream truck that's gone missing across the city in the last two weeks. This is serious.'

'You bet it's serious.' Leo smacked his fist into his palm. 'And serious stuff is just the thing for Fixit International Inc., right, Isaac? . . . Isaac?'

Leo poked the mound of metal and shook his head. He went outside to the woodpile. He found a good chunk of wood, grabbed the axe and split it into bits.

Ragnar, his pet pig, watched and yawned.

'Not going to help, are you?' Leo asked as he gathered the firewood.

'Nope,' Ragnar said. 'Can't pick up wood with these trotters.'

'If you can't help, you can't be part of Fixit International Inc.'

'I can answer the phone, solve complicated maths problems and do internet searches, stuff like that.' Ragnar followed Leo back into the shed.

Leo opened a door in the pile of metal, fanned smoke away, then stuffed some wood inside. The pile of metal shook, then sat up straight. It stretched its arms, wobbled its head, stood and shimmied a little. A few bolts fell off and made pinging noises as they bounced on the concrete floor.

'How's that, Isaac?' Leo asked. 'Better?'

'I should have been more careful,' Isaac said. 'I nearly let my fire burn out.'

Isaac was an ancient, wood-burning robot. He'd belonged to Leo's great-great-grandfather. When Leo found him in a crate under the house he was almost a solid lump of rust. It took ages to get him working again.

'And what were you saying about ice-cream?' he asked the wise, old robot.

'It looks as if someone is stealing all the ice-cream in the entire city.'

'*All* the ice-cream?' Ragnar squealed. 'It's the end of the world!'

CHAPTER 2

'Don't worry, Ragnar,' Leo said. 'International Fixit Inc. is on the case. Screen, Isaac.'

Isaac clanked over to the wall of the shed. He reached for the paint-spattered tarpaulin. 'Oh my!' he cried, grabbing his back.

'You okay, Isaac?' Leo asked. 'Is the rust coming back?'

'Just a tad. I'll need some oil soon.'

The robot swayed a little and reached up again, more slowly this time. The tarpaulin fell to the ground to reveal a map of the world.

Leo was proud of his SlinkyScope. It was his command viewer and it was vital to the activities of Fixit International Inc. It displayed almost any scene he needed. He'd made it out of dozens of slinkys plus some quantum spark colliders. He liked it, especially when it did that wavy-wiggly thing.

'This is what's happening.' Isaac pointed at a location on the map. 'Ice-cream trucks have gone missing here, here, here and here.'

Each time he touched the SlinkyScope, a red light flared.

'I see a pattern,' Ragnar said. 'They're all red.'

'Keep it up, Ragnar,' Leo warned, 'and you'll get to wear the Obvious Hat.'

Ragnar glanced at the hat in the corner of the shed. It was tall, pointy and dusted with fairy glitter. He shuddered. 'No, thanks. Not for this porker.'

Isaac tapped the SlinkyScope. 'I've been getting reports that supermarkets are running low on ice-cream supplies too, so it's not just the trucks.'

'This is serious.' Leo rubbed his chin. 'You don't think it could be . . .?'

'I do,' Isaac said. His glowing eyes were troubled.

'What?' Ragnar said. 'What is it, you guys?'

Leo shook his fist. 'This could be the work of the diabolical Ice-cream Domination League.'

'You mean the guys who want to build a giant robot out of spaghetti?' Ragnar said. 'No, sorry, that's the Masters of Pasta.' He wrinkled his snout. 'Remind me about the Ice-cream Domination League again?'

Leo marched in a tight circle, his hands behind his back, thinking hard. 'It's a ruthless organisation dedicated to owning all the ice-cream in the world.'

Ragnar's ears pricked up at this. 'Even mango?'

'Even mango,' Isaac confirmed.

Ragnar shook his head. 'There's so much evil in the world.'

'Leonardo!' His mother's voice sailed across the backyard. 'Want a lift to school or are you catching the bus?'

'Lift!' Leo pointed at Isaac, then at Ragnar. 'We'll follow up on this after school.'

'Sure thing,' Ragnar said. 'Go and learn something, eh?'

Isaac waved as Leo raced towards the door. 'One thing, young sir. Wild Wilbur left a message scrawled in chalk on the path. It said that nothing would stop his revenge.'

'No time for that now, Isaac,' Leo called over his shoulder. 'I've got learning to do.'

CHAPTER 3

'How was school, Leonardo?'

His mum was tapping away on her laptop. Probably trying to save another major Hollywood studio with her financial magic, Leo guessed.

'Not bad, Mum.'

'What did you do?'

Leo thought about it. It had been a normal school day, except that one of his classmates had kept asking annoying questions about Fixit International Inc. 'Nothing much. I taught the teachers about advanced weapons systems and top-grade cybersecurity.'

'That's nice.'

'I'll be out in the shed.'

'Take a piece of fruit with you.'

Leo grabbed an apple and hurried to the shed. He jiggled the lock, then marched through the knee-deep plans and sketches. He pushed aside a crate full of glass eyes. He found a stool he'd made out of a water cooler and sat on it.

'Isaac! Ragnar!' he called. 'Fixit International Inc. has work to do!'

A cupboard under the painting bench opened. Ragnar poked his head out. 'More work,' he moaned. 'I mean, it wouldn't hurt if you had some friends. They could help out, make it easier, let me spend more time in my mud pit.'

Leo didn't answer. He put his apple on the bench, then brushed the blank sheet of paper in front of him. Ragnar's words had hit him hard.

Leonardo da Vinci, the inventor of the incredible, had never really had a friend. He knew lots of people, but there was never anyone close. Oh, he had a robot and a talking pig, but they weren't *people*.

Leo had been too busy saving the world to worry about this friend thing. Friends seemed to take up a lot of time. People with friends didn't invent amazing devices. People with friends ate popcorn and watched movies instead of searching for the best way to paint people in realistic but interesting poses. People with friends laughed at cat videos together instead of looking for ways to stop the supervillains.

Leo knew most of his fellow students thought he was a bit strange. Perhaps it was the way he liked to use plasticine to build models of multistorey hide-outs with secret basements and shark pools. Maybe it was because he did rough portraits over and over and never finished a good copy. Maybe it was because he forgot people's names. He once suggested that everyone should write their name on their forehead to make it easier for him.

Maybe he *was* just a little bit strange, he thought.

A knock came at the door of Fixit International Inc. Leonardo da Vinci, loner and battler against evil, wasn't sure what to do.

He looked at Isaac, who shrugged.

He looked at Ragnar, who said, 'Are you going to eat that apple? And why don't you answer the door?'

Leo wrestled with the lock. When he finally opened the door, he couldn't believe who was there. It was his classmate from Vinci Primary School, the one who'd been asking all the annoying questions.

'What do you want?' Leo asked. He'd never really got the hang of polite greetings.

The girl looked back at him evenly. She was a little taller than Leo and had a mass of wavy black hair, which was tied back with a red ribbon. She had a nose that was in the middle of her face and her ears were on both sides of her head. Leo thought about sketching her standing with her arms outstretched. He'd draw a circle right around her, too. Yeah, that'd look just perfect.

'I want to join International Fixit Inc.'

'How did you know this shed was the headquarters of Fixit International Inc.?' Leo demanded.

'There's a sign on the door and one on the roof. You've got one out by the letterbox, too. Not to mention that your address is on your website.'

Leo made a mental note to have words with Ragnar. The location of International Fixit Inc. was supposed to be a *secret*. 'We don't need any new members right now.'

'Why? How many have you got?'

'One. Plus a wood-burning robot and a talking pig.'

She clapped her hands together. 'So there's plenty of room.'

'Why should I let you become a member?'

The visitor held up a roll of duct tape and a hammer. 'I like fixing things.'

Leo rubbed his chin. This newcomer certainly knew what International Fixit Inc. was all about. 'All right, you've convinced me,' he said. 'What's your name?'

'Mina.' She hopped from one foot to the other in excitement. 'Does this mean I'm in?'

'You're on probation.'

'So what do I have to do to prove myself?'

'Just be useful. Fixit International Inc. doesn't need useless.'

'Okay, I'll start by repairing the lock on this door.'

'I've been meaning to get around to that one.'

'Won't take me long.'

'Go to it, Probationary Member Mina.'

Mina grinned. 'Do I need to salute or something?'

'Just fix the lock.'

Mina grinned some more. 'One thing, though . . .'

'Yes, Probationary Member Mina?'

'What's the "Inc." stand for in Fixit International Inc.?'

'It just sounds good. Got a problem with that?'

'Nope. It's really cool.'

Cool? Leo blinked. He'd never been called cool before.

He liked it.

CHAPTER 4

Leo introduced Mina to Isaac and Ragnar. Mina stared. 'A real robot. That's amazing!'

'And what am I?' Ragnar said. 'Mr Boring Talking Pig?'

'Hey, you're amazing too,' Mina said. She looked around. 'In fact, this is all amazing!'

'If she keeps that sort of thing up, she could be a candidate for the Obvious Hat,' Ragnar muttered to Isaac.

They both looked at the hat in the corner with dread.

All that afternoon, Leo, Isaac and Ragnar sketched plans, made lists and searched for information about what the Ice-cream Domination League was up to.

Mina used half a roll of duct tape repairing things that needed repairing. She also listened and made suggestions. Some of them weren't bad.

Finally, Leo called her over to the main workbench in front of the SlinkyScope.

'We've had some developments, haven't we, Isaac?'

Isaac pointed at the SlinkyScope. 'The

entire ice-cream fleet has disappeared. There is not a single truck left on the road.'

'In the middle of a heatwave, too,' Mina groaned. She squinted at the SlinkyScope. 'That resolution looks a bit off. I'll get a screwdriver.'

'Not now,' Leo said. 'Ragnar, anything to report?'

'Nope, except that I'm starving.'

Leo went to the SlinkyScope. 'The Ice-cream Domination League must have a plan. We only have one hope to stop it before it gets out of control.' He tapped the screen and it shivered with a metallic ringing. 'Just here, on the edge of Vinci, is the biggest ice-cream factory in the world. Right, Isaac?'

'Correct,' Isaac replied. 'Each day, Vinci

Ice-cream Works makes enough ice-cream to stretch from here to the moon.'

'Stretchy ice-cream,' Mina said. 'Now that's something I'd like to see.'

Leo frowned, then jotted down a few numbers on a scrap of paper. 'Stretchy ice-cream. Cold and creamy but snappy like gum . . .'

A noisy *tap-tap-tapping* at the window interrupted them. A pigeon was at the glass and it rapped again with its beak.

Mina edged to the window, making sure she didn't trip over the wires, lengths of pipe and a model of the Eiffel Tower. She eased the window open. 'Steady, little fella,' she whispered before grabbing the pigeon.

'Let me get the message tied around its leg,' Isaac said.

The robot climbed over the box of old toasters, leapt over a pile of doughnut holers and squeezed between the battered dog sled and the Little Buddy Cyclone Generator. Very carefully, he untied the message capsule from the pigeon's leg.

'It's for you, young sir,' he said to Leo. 'It's from Wild Wilbur.'

Leo read it. 'He says he's on his way and that I'll regret what I did to him.'

'After you sent him to supervillain prison, didn't he promise to turn into a good guy?' Ragnar asked.

Leo shook his head. 'You can't trust super-villains these days.'

'I wouldn't call him a supervillain,' Ragnar said. 'I mean, he's nowhere near as deadly as

Lorna the Perilous or the Uber-Overlord. He's more of a mildly strong villain.'

Mina let go of the pigeon and it flew off.

'He's not anything like the Edge of Darkness,' Isaac pointed out. 'Now there was a *real* supervillain.'

'Oh, yeah,' Ragnar said. 'The Edge of Darkness. Great costume. Very stylish.'

'You realise that they're all in prison, thanks to us?' Leo said.

'Which means we've got some dandy enemies,' Ragnar said. 'But don't let that worry you, Mina.'

'Although, it probably helps to know the sorts of superenemies we're dealing with here,' Isaac added.

'Superenemies,' Mina breathed. 'Wow. I have superenemies.'

'International Fixit Inc. has superenemies,' Leo corrected. 'You're just a probationary member.'

'So I have probationary superenemies.' Mina's eyes were bright. 'It's still pretty amazing.'

Isaac raised a finger to speak but it fell off. He had trouble finding it as it had landed in a box of old plumbing tools. Finally, he screwed it back on and pointed it at Leo. 'I think Vinci Ice-cream Works is the perfect place for an ambush.'

Leo held up the plan he'd been working on. The paper was covered with sketches of roads, buildings, fences and explosions. He'd taken a lot of care with the explosions. 'Exactly,' he said.

Mina danced up and down on the spot. 'Sounds like fun.'

'They'll be waiting for us,' Leo warned. 'We'll have to go in hard, so if anyone's got a problem with that, speak up now.'

Mina glanced at her phone. 'I don't have a problem with it, but I've got to be at basketball practice in an hour. Can this wait until tomorrow?'

'Is that the time?' Leo yelped, running for the door. 'I have homework!'

'We have homework?' Mina said.

Leo skidded to a stop. 'Correct. *We* have maths homework.'

Mina groaned. 'So I've got basketball and then maths. Great.'

'We'll have to sort out the ambush tomorrow,' Leo said. 'You know, I almost feel sorry for the Ice-cream Domination League.'

CHAPTER 5

Leo's father walked him to the bus stop the next morning. 'Why don't you bring your friend to the restaurant for dinner tonight?' he said as they waited side by side in the sun.

'Friend?' Leo said. 'What friend?'

'The one that was using duct tape to fix the antenna on the roof of the shed.'

'Oh, that's Probationary Member Mina. She's on trial.'

'On trial as a friend?'

'On trial as a member of Fixit International Inc. She's not bad with a hammer.'

'I see.' Leo's dad put his hands in his pockets. 'So how about it?'

Leo liked eating in his father's restaurant, but would Mina? 'We're pretty busy,' he said with a shrug.

'Uh-huh.'

'We've got to ambush a major crime gang and stop them from taking over the world's supply of a dessert favourite.'

'That'll keep you busy, all right.' His dad scratched his beard.

Leo thought he looked like a pirate. He'd sketched him a few dozen times with a parrot on his shoulder because it looked right.

'Just wanted to let you know you can bring a friend around for a feed anytime you like.'

'Thanks, Dad.'

CHAPTER 6

Leo had trouble concentrating at school all that day. His mind kept drifting to plans of attack and his Kitties HiLo notebook was littered with doodles of fallback strategies.

Kitties HiLo was one of Leo's major creations. He still couldn't believe that the cartoons made him the millions of dollars that he poured into Fixit International Inc. They were the two cutest cat characters in the world, the bestest of friends, one big, one small, with extra smiley faces. Leo thought they were annoying, but he was about the only person in the whole universe who thought that. It was hard to go for more than a microsecond without seeing the two dinky characters on a backpack, a drink bottle or a hi-vis vest. Construction workers were the biggest fans of the two kitties.

Leo was grateful to Kitties HiLo, but he did get tired of having to come up with new cat sketches. Today, though, he was planning an ambush. He filled page after page with maps, plans, diagrams and equations.

'Leonardo da Vinci, time to wake up.'

Leo blinked and looked around. 'Sorry?'

His teacher smiled at him and shook her head. 'Or are you daydreaming again?'

'Sorry, Ms Tempany.'

'I don't know how you can keep drifting off like that and still be so far ahead,' she said.

'I suppose I read a lot . . .'

Ms Tempany laughed. 'Well, whatever you're doing, just keep it up.'

'Yes, Ms Tempany.'

She moved on, and Leo went back to planning a sure-fire supervillain trap.

'We have to be prepared,' Leo said to Mina as they walked home from the bus stop.

'You mean weapons and stuff?' Mina whooped and clapped her hands. 'At head-quarters I saw something called a SuperSilly String Cannon. Can I use that one?'

Leo was proud of the SuperSilly String Cannon. 'Go ahead.'

'Cool!' Mina said. 'And what are you going to use?'

'The Ice-cream Domination League means business. I think it's time to break out the Crispinator.'

'Sounds deadly. What's it do?'

'Do? It crisps, that's what it does . . .' Leo thought back to the last time he used the Crispinator, when he had cornered the Massive Mangler. The giant supervillain had gone on a rampage through the centre of town. He'd pulled down buildings, ripped up roads and punched a huge hole in the side of the Vinci Gardening Club.

Leo had taken the Massive Mangler down with some well-placed shots from the SuperSilly String Cannon. When the giant struggled, the SuperSilly String stopped stretching and locked in place. All Leo had had to do was use the Crispinator to stun him and then he'd have been able to turn the Massive Mangler over to authorities.

But it all went wrong. Leo had made the weapon out of hair dryers, a sandwich maker and a miniature thorium nuclear reactor. It was an insanely complicated piece of machinery. But when the time came to blast the massive supervillain, Leo couldn't find the 'on' switch.

He'd forgotten to include one.

While the Massive Mangler struggled, Leo had fumbled. He'd sweated. He'd searched. He'd twisted nozzles. He'd adjusted slide covers. Then he accidentally broke off one of the pyro-flanges and the Crispinator fell apart.

'Noooooooo!' he'd cried, dropping to his knees.

Luckily, the Massive Mangler didn't get away – no thanks to Leonardo da Vinci. The giant tripped on a bus and knocked himself out.

Leo shivered at the memory, even though they were still in a heatwave. This failure haunted him. Sometimes he woke up in the middle of the night because of it. Sometimes, too, he woke up in the middle of the night because Ragnar liked to poke him with a piece of wood for a laugh, but that was different.

Leo now had a chance to make good. After repairs – including a really, really good 'on/off' switch – he was determined to use the Crispinator. This time it would work.

'Leo?' Mina waved a hand in front of his face. 'You've gone all zombie dreamy.'

Leo smacked his fist into his palm. 'With the plan I've worked out, this ambush will be a piece of cake.'

Ragnar was waiting for them at the front gate. 'You guys got cake? Mmm, cake. Let's eat cake before we go and thump these villains, hey? Cake? Cake?'

'Supervillains first,' Leo said. 'Cake later.'

'Fair enough,' the pig grumbled, 'but it had better be good cake.'

CHAPTER 7

Inside, Isaac was using a screwdriver to tighten one of his knees. They said hello to him, then Leo took Mina to the Small Lift.

'How far down does it go?' Mina asked.

'Far enough,' Leo said mysteriously.

He thought it was good to be mysterious sometimes.

Mina just nodded as the doors opened and they stepped inside. 'Great.'

Leo frowned. Maybe he wasn't mysterious enough. Maybe he should try some mysterious laughter or something.

The Small Lift pinged. They had reached Basement Level 5. Lights came on and revealed a long line of shapes covered in tarpaulins.

Leo led Mina over to the nearest one and whipped away the tarpaulin. 'Behold the Strikebird!' He waited. 'I'm not hearing any gasps of astonishment.'

'I'm too amazed to be astonished,' Mina said. 'And I don't like gasping – asthma.'

'Okay, just as long as you're impressed.'

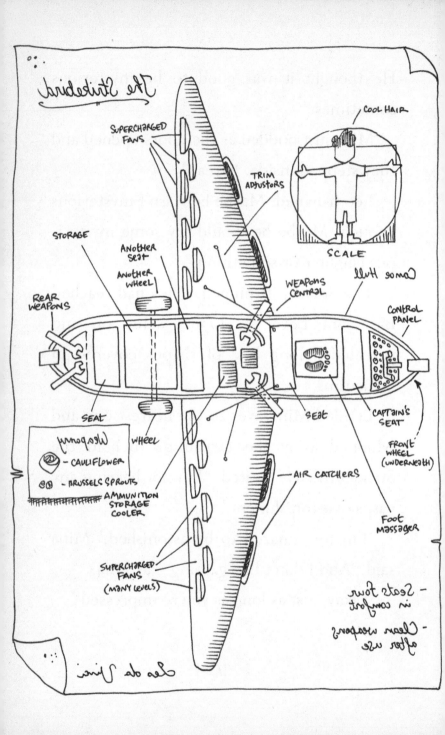

Mina stuck her hands in her pockets. She walked around the Strikebird and let out a low whistle. 'It looks like a canoe,' she said. 'A canoe with wings and wheels.'

'Well, it started as a canoe but we made improvements. Didn't we, Isaac?'

Isaac clanked out of the Small Lift, with Ragnar following along. The robot bowed and puffed some smoke. 'We certainly did. Once we attached the dozens of supercharged fans, the canoe became a vehicle capable of moving at super-hyper-ultra-speed. It can travel on the ground, under water and through the air. It's remarkable.'

'It also has an in-built foot massager,' Leo added. 'Now, everyone aboard!' he ordered. 'Isaac, you stay here and monitor the SlinkyScope.'

'Shall do,' the robot replied. 'Don't be late. Your dad is making butter chicken for dinner.'

'Butter chicken?' Leo's mouth started to water. 'Excellent!'

Ragnar hesitated. 'Look, I'd better stay . . . to keep an eye on Isaac.'

Leo raised an eyebrow. 'And so you can get a head start on the butter chicken?'

Ragnar sniffed, and since he was a pig with a snout the size of pie dish, it was a magnificent sniff. 'I don't know what you mean.'

'No time for that now.' Leo piled into the seat at the front of the command module. He flipped a few switches and pushed a few buttons. The Strikebird trembled. 'Helmets on!'

'Helmets?' Mina asked. 'What helmets?'

'Under your seat.' Leo tried to speak clearly and calmly, like a real pilot. 'Safety first.'

'This is a bike helmet,' Mina said, holding hers up. 'Shouldn't we be wearing Strikebird helmets?'

'Write "Strikebird" on it if you like.' Leo threw her a permanent marker. 'Fixit International Inc., here we go!'

The Strikebird rolled past the Small Lift, towards the Really Big Lift. Once they were inside and the doors hissed closed, cheesy music filled the Really Big Lift.

'The music was Ragnar's idea,' Leo explained, noticing Mina's puzzled expression. 'He has horrible taste.'

When the doors hissed open, they were on a giant platform well above the roof of the shed.

'Time to take to the air,' Leo said. 'Just pay attention to the safety demonstration and make sure your seatbelt is fastened.'

'Huh?'

'Hold on!'

CHAPTER 8

The Strikebird sprang into the air, all fans blasting. Even though Leo knew what was coming, it felt as if he'd left his stomach behind on the launch pad. He hoped that it would catch up soon, because he didn't like feeling stomach-less.

Mina cheered as the Strikebird swooped towards Vinci Ice-cream Works. 'Keep an eye on the structural integrity, Probationary Member Mina,' Leo shouted over the noise of the fans.

'Sure thing!' Mina shouted back. 'I brought a hammer, some duct tape and a spray pack of oil. I'm ready for any emergency.'

'Can you handle Weapons Central as well?' Leo veered to the right to avoid a crow. It sneered at them as they whooshed past.

'Weapons Central?' Mina shouted. 'You bet!'

'Check out your control panel,' Leo responded, 'and be ready.'

'So many buttons,' Mina shouted. 'Couldn't you afford a zipper?'

'What?'

'Just joking, Leo! Buttons, zippers, you know.'

'No time for joking,' Leo growled. 'This is serious! Ready the Brussels Sprouts Cannon and the Heat-seeking Cauliflower Missiles. We'll hit them where it hurts.'

'Aren't vegetables meant to be good for you?'

'Maybe, but we'll see how the Ice-cream Domination League likes being bombarded with turnips.'

Leo kicked the flaps, nudged the trim adjustors, elbowed the air catchers and pushed the wheel down. The Strikebird dived like an eagle.

'Yahooooooooooooooooo!' Mina whooped.

The Vinci Ice-cream Works was a big cube of a building seven or eight storeys high.

The roof was flat and white. The Strikebird levelled out and screamed around it in a circle.

Huge doors in the side of the factory burst open. A truck raced out. It was dark purple with plenty of chrome. The setting sun made it look as if it were on fire.

Leo narrowed his eyes. 'I think we've found them!'

'How do you know?'

'Purple is the favourite colour of the IDL,' Leo shouted. 'Besides, it has its initials in big letters on the side.'

'Boom! That's good noticing, Leo!'

'Weapons Central, fire at will!'

The Strikebird shook. Hundreds of brussels sprouts screamed towards the purple truck at twice the speed of sound.

Leo smiled grimly.

When the sprouts struck the truck, it skidded sideways and almost crashed into the fence. Its engine roared and its back wheels spun until they smoked. Then the truck launched itself towards the gate.

'They're getting away!' Mina cried. 'You want me to fix anything?'

'Not just yet, Probationary Member Mina! It's time for the Zucchini Interceptors!'

'You got it!'

The Strikebird kicked eight times as Mina launched eight massive zucchini. They streaked towards the truck as it neared the open gate. One by one, they smacked into the truck's windscreen. Green-yellow pulp sprayed all over the rogue vehicle.

The truck screeched, bucked, buckled and

jackknifed. It came to a stop, blocking the
open gate.

'Good job, Probationary Member Mina!'
Leo said. 'I think we've done it. I always said
that the forces of evil are hopeless, especially
when they come up against International
Fixit –'

'Look out!' Mina shouted. 'Forces of evil!'

The rear doors of the truck had banged open and a horde of purple-clad figures was swarming out. Some jumped up and down angrily. Some shook their fists angrily. Some took their helmets off and threw them on the ground and kicked them angrily.

But Leo wasn't worried about them. He was worried about the ones who had dangerous-looking pipes on their shoulders and who were aiming them angrily.

The Strikebird shuddered. Alarms went off, and Leo winced. He'd wanted to have really good alarms like in the movies – those big *gah-gah-gah* ones that mean some major explosion is about to happen. He would have been happy with the *ah-oogah-ah-oogah* alarms you find in nuclear facilities, but he'd had to settle for the alarm out of a clock radio.

It was embarrassing, really.

'We're hit!' Mina called out. She already had her duct tape and hammer in her hands. 'I think it was chocolate or raspberry ripple – one or the other.'

'We're going in!' Leo cried. 'Brace yourself!'

CHAPTER
9

Leo wrestled with the controls. He hauled
back on the stick. He was jolted hard when the
plane hit. It screeched and threw up sparks as
it skidded along the concrete. Eventually, Leo
brought it to a halt in front of the ice-cream
factory.

Mina was the first out of the Strikebird. Her SuperSilly String Cannon was locked and loaded. Leo leapt out right behind her with his Crispinator, only to slip in a puddle of melted ice-cream that had dripped from the ruined Strikebird. He protected the Crispinator as he fell but that meant he landed right on his backside.

'Don't worry about me,' he snapped when a grinning Mina went to help him up. 'We're in a danger zone. Stay alert.'

'Okay, but we'd better move away before the Strikebird bursts into flames.'

'It's not going to burst into flames,' Leo said. 'That only happens in the movies.'

'It's not?' Mina looked disappointed.

'No,' Leo said, fumbling in his back pocket. 'The Strikebird won't burst into flames unless

I press this remote with the "burst into flames" button on it.'

Mina peered at the device in his hand. 'How would you know if the button has been pressed?'

'Easy. It'd be flat.'

'Um, it looks flat to me.'

'Don't be ridicu—' Leo looked, then looked again. The 'burst into flames' button was completely flat. 'Run!'

While they ran, Mina couldn't stop laughing. 'You fell on it, right?' Mina laughed some more. 'You should have seen your face!'

Behind them, the Strikebird burst into flames. Leo ground his teeth. That was the ninth supervehicle he'd lost in battles with supervillains. They owed him.

He and Mina rounded the corner of the

building to find dozens of purple figures screaming towards them. Leo snarled. Here was his chance to collect a little bit of what supervillains owed him.

Mina dropped to one knee and started pumping the SuperSilly String Cannon. A web of multicoloured SuperSilly String sprang from the triple-barrelled weapon. The IDL minions were immediately tangled in the sticky, stretchy stuff. Their cries of triumph became cries of crying.

'Sooky babies!' Mina shouted. 'That'll teach you to mess with International Fixit Inc.!'

Another wave of purple minions poured out of the truck and ran towards them, screaming. Mina fired again and again. 'Take that, you violet vermin!'

'Good shooting, Probationary Member Mina!' Leo cried. 'And excellent taunting!'

Leo held off using the Crispinator for a while. Not because he didn't trust it, he told himself. He just wanted to see what Probationary Member Mina was made of.

'This SuperSilly String Cannon is amazing!' Mina sprayed more IDL minions. The driveway in front of them was a mess of shouting, writhing purple figures covered in rainbow threads. 'I like the pair of fluffy dice on the trigger guard, too!'

Leo shrugged. He never could resist splicing stuff onto his inventions. 'There's no reason a superweapon can't look good.'

'You know what else is looking good?' a voice said from behind them. 'Me.'

Now *that* was a supervillain quip if Leo

had ever heard one! He swung around. A purple-clad figure was pointing a rotating quintuple-barrelled weapon at them. She was wearing a Leader of the Ice-cream Domination League hat. As she marched towards them Leo saw the Leader of the Ice-cream Domination League badge on her tunic, the Leader of the Ice-cream Domination League belt buckle and the Leader of the Ice-cream Domination League shoelaces.

Leo had finally come face to face with the mysterious Leader of the Ice-cream Domination League.

CHAPTER 10

The Leader of the IDL looked a lot like an ordinary ten-year-old girl – but the way she was holding that quintuple-barrelled weapon meant she was a supervillain, sure enough.

'Don't move,' she said. 'This weapon fires vanilla, strawberry and chocolate *plus* it has two barrels for gelato. Throw down your weapons.'

Mina lowered the SuperSilly String Cannon, but Leo had other ideas. 'I don't think so,' he said.

This was it. This was his big chance. He'd practised for hours. He was sure he could fire the Crispinator before the Leader of the Ice-cream Domination League could fire her ice-cream cannon. Besides, the scorching blast of the Crispinator would melt the ice-cream, easy.

So why were his palms so sweaty? Why was his heart thundering in his chest? Why were his knees wobbling?

The Leader of the IDL glared at him. He glared at the Leader of the IDL. Mina looked at a butterfly that was fluttering past.

Leo's phone rang.

Leo had done some tweaking to his phone. It was possibly the most powerful handheld device in the world. It was vacuum-proof, waterproof, dinosaur-proof and wirelessly connected to most of the machines of International Fixit Inc. It also had lots of ringtones, and he'd programmed this one especially. He held up a hand. 'Wait, wait. It's my mum.'

The Leader of the Ice-cream Domination League lowered her massive weapon.

Leo listened. 'Dinner's on the table?' He glanced at the Leader of the Ice-cream Domination League. 'I'm a bit busy right now.'

The Leader of the Ice-cream Domination League shook her head. 'It's okay,' she mimed.

'Thanks,' Leo mimed in return. 'I'll be

there straight away,' he said into the phone, then hung up and slipped his phone back into his pocket. 'Thanks,' he said to the Leader of the IDL – aloud this time.

'Don't mention it,' she replied. 'Anyway, we can pick this up tomorrow.'

'After school,' Leo reminded her.

'Of course.' She paused. 'What are you having for dinner?'

'Butter chicken.'

'Yum.'

'You?'

'Sardines on toast.'

'Sorry about that.'

'I happen to like sardines. They're very good for you.' The Leader of the Ice-cream Domination League saluted and hurried off.

'I'm glad about that,' Mina said. 'It's getting

late and Mum and Dad will be wondering where I am.'

'Battling evil and saving the world is important,' Leo said, 'but you do have to fit it into the rest of your day.'

'Makes sense. What's the point in fixing the world if you're messing up the rest of the world while you do it?'

A vehicle pulled up to the gate. Leo was pleased to see Isaac at the wheel of the Megaslasher. It didn't just have a cool name, it was one of Leo's most reliable inventions. The Megaslasher was a ride-on lawnmower with a trailer, to which he'd bolted on parts from a keyboard synthesiser so that it played tunes whenever the wheels moved.

Ragnar waved at the ruins of the Strikebird. 'I guess this means no cake, right?'

Leo didn't answer. He was too busy looking at the sky. Big white letters were being written against the blueness: *Leonardo da Vinci! Your time is nearly up! I will get you! Wild Wiblur.*

Leo smacked his fist into his palm. 'Wild Wilbur!'

Mina shook her head. 'He misspelled his own name?'

'Wild Wilbur never could spell,' Leo said. 'It didn't stop him from becoming my sixth deadliest villain, though.'

'I remember when he was just a lowly twelfth deadliest villain,' Ragnar declared. 'But he had ambition. He's worked his way up and I think he has an eye on fifth spot.'

'Maybe,' Leo said slowly, then shook his head. 'No time for that – butter chicken awaits!'

CHAPTER 11

The next day Leo waited for Mina outside the school so they could head back to the ice-cream factory.

His stomach growled.

Leo had always had a noisy stomach. It was the sort of noisy stomach that made people look around for a lion on the loose. Right now it was growling so loudly that people were staring. Some put their hands over their ears. Others were running away, shouting, 'Lion!'

It was all because Leo was After-school Hungry.

Leo had done some thinking about this. He'd decided that After-school Hungry was one of the most powerful things in the universe. After-school Hungry was to ordinary hungry as an elephant was to a flea. After-school Hungry was a raging beast that turned you into some sort of reverse super-hero, one who'd bite a radioactive spider instead of the other way around, just in case it was tasty.

Leo had even made a graph where ordinary hungry was a nice blue bar on one side and

next to it was After-school Hungry. After-school Hungry went right off the chart. He tried making it into a pie chart but that made things worse because mmm . . . pie.

He wiped the drool off his chin just before Mina hurried up to him.

'Let's go,' she said as Isaac and Ragnar clanked and trotted towards them.

Isaac had the portable SlinkyScope in one hand. With the other hand, he waved. It fell off, but Ragnar caught it in his mouth.

'Greetings, fellow Fixit Internationals!' Isaac said. 'We must be careful. We've been monitoring much activity at the ice-cream factory. Haven't we, Ragnar?'

'Mrmgrmphllblrp,' Ragnar said.

Isaac took his hand from Ragnar and screwed it back on. 'Sorry.'

Ragnar wiped his mouth with a trotter. 'You taste terrible, Isaac. So greasy!'

'It keeps away the rust,' Isaac replied primly.

'You can pick up your own hand in future,' Ragnar said. 'Sheesh.'

'No time for arguing,' Leo said. 'And thanks for the warning, Isaac, but we have a battle to get to.'

The street ahead was long and lined with factories, warehouses and clearance centres. It took them around a bend or two and through some tall trees before they could see the Vinci Ice-cream Works. But before they reached it, they couldn't.

The road was blocked with barriers and flashing lights. Lots of yellow-and-black tape, too. Zigzaggy sheets of metal were stuck in between signs that read: *DANGER! DEMOLITION IN PROGRESS! EXPLOSIONS AND OTHER NASTY STUFF, SO STAY BACK, RIGHT BACK. DON'T EVEN THINK OF COMING CLOSE OR ELSE YOU'LL . . .*

'They ran out of sign,' Ragnar said.

'It could be continued on the back,' Mina said, 'but I really don't want to know what we're else-ing.'

A warning siren sounded, loud enough to drown out Leo's stomach growls. Mina put her hands over her ears. Ragnar squealed in pain. Isaac hummed along with it.

Leo marched up to the barriers and searched for the source of the siren.

It was coming from the Vinci Ice-cream Works.

Leo's mouth fell open. His stomach, sensing that it might have a chance to break free, let loose a rip-roaring growl, but at that moment the ice-cream factory blew up.

Now, Leo had watched about a million hours of chimneys and buildings being demolished on YouTube, so he could tell that whoever had blown up the ice-cream factory was pretty good at it.

There was no sheet of flame. There was no fountain of fire. There was no billowing black smoke. The Vinci Ice-cream Works simply gave up the fight against gravity. Its walls sagged, then slumped, then fell inward with a thunderous crash.

A tidal wave of dust rolled from the site.

'Duck!' Leo called to his friends.

'No, I'm a pig,' Ragnar huffed. A shadow fell across them, and he looked up to see what it was. 'Oh.'

'Ouch, ouch, ouch!' Leo cried, copping a gob full of grit.

He closed his eyes. He could hear others blundering around nearby. He dropped to his hands and knees and started crawling.

When the last of the dust blew past, he rolled over and sat up, panting. He watched the dust wave bowl down the street, just as if it were on the way to do some shopping.

'The ice-cream factory's gone!' Mina gasped.

Leo climbed to his feet and wiped the dirt from his face. He scrambled over the roadblock and trudged to the gates of the ice-cream factory.

A huge pile of concrete, metal and glass was all that was left of Vinci Ice-cream Works.

CHAPTER 12

'Why would they do that?' Leo muttered as he surveyed the ruins of the ice-cream factory. 'They're the Ice-cream Domination League, not the Ice-cream Demolition League.'

Ragnar stamped a trotter. 'If the Ice-cream Domination League blows up the biggest ice-cream factory in the world, that means they must have some other source of ice-cream.'

'Good point.' Leo whirled and pointed. 'Isaac, what other sources of ice-cream does the Ice-cream Domination League have?'

'Hold on a moment, sir,' the robot replied. 'I'm having some trouble with the portable SlinkyScope. Hmm. The answer is none.'

'They haven't taken over any other factories?'

'No, they've just blown them all up.'

Leo blinked. He hadn't been expecting *that*. For years, the IDL had been trying to take over the global ice-cream industry and now they'd blown up all the ice-cream factories?

'It doesn't make sense,' Mina said.

'I was just thinking that,' Leo said.

Mina grinned. 'I know. You were thinking out loud.'

News helicopters were buzzing overhead. Leo looked up, and for a second he thought about designing a helicopter with a big spiral corkscrew instead of a rotor, but he pushed the idea to the back of his mind. 'The IDL must have a plan,' he said.

'They could be making it up as they go along,' Mina suggested. She was eyeing the huge mound of rubble as if she wanted to go and repair it.

'The Leader of the IDL isn't crazy,' Ragnar scoffed. 'Well, she might be crazy, but she's not *crazy*, if you know what I mean.'

Isaac hurried over, smoke puffing from

his chimney. 'The portable SlinkyScope has something.'

They all crowded around it. The flubbery screen shook and trembled, then cleared to reveal a figure standing against a white background. She wore a snappy violet suit, and she'd pushed her hat back on her head. She was looking very, very pleased with herself.

'The Ice-cream Domination League has taken over the North Pole,' she announced. 'We will use our superior freezer-based technology to resist any efforts to remove us.'

The scene cut away to show lots and lots of white.

'I'm guessing that's the North Pole,' Ragnar said.

The whiteness burst into flurries. Dozens of shiny, white vehicles emerged. Some launched into the sky. Some splashed into the water. Others ploughed around and around in circles, sending up huge sprays of snow and scaring nearby walruses.

Everyone looked at Leo. 'I'm convinced,' he said, 'that they'd be planes, ships and tanks made of ice.'

'Ice,' Mina echoed. 'Oh, that's the freezer-based technology that she was talking about.'

One of the tanks had stopped. A small violet figure was standing next to it. The camera zoomed in on the Leader of the Ice-cream Domination League standing with her fists on her hips.

For a second, Leo had an idea for a tank of his own. He could see it. It would be round, pointy on the top and really fast. He made a mental note for later and, using an estimation

of the height of the Leader of IDL, did a quick calculation in his head. 'That tank must be thirty metres in height,' he concluded.

'Our icy defences cannot be beaten,' the Leader of the IDL declared. 'Leave us alone and do not attempt to build any new ice-cream factories. We are the Ice-cream Domination League. Have a nice day.'

The screen went black.

Leo smashed his fist into his palm. 'They must be making ice-cream at the North Pole, which they'll sell for zillions of dollars.' He shook his head. 'No, it can't be. What do you need to make ice-cream?'

'Cream?' Ragnar answered.

'Sugar and flavourings?' Mina added.

'Right,' Leo said. 'And I know for certain that there aren't many cows at the North Pole. So, unless they plan to use polar bear milk, they're stuck.'

For a second he considered creating a machine for milking polar bears, but he pushed it aside. 'They *must* have a plan,' he muttered to himself.

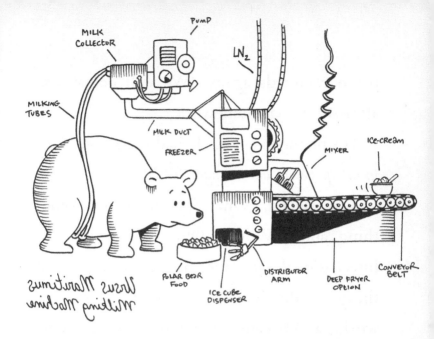

MILK COLLECTOR

PUMP

LN₂

MILKING TUBES

MILK DUCT

FREEZER

MIXER

ICE-CREAM

POLAR BEAR FOOD

ICE CUBE DISPENSER

DISTRIBUTOR ARM

DEEP FRYER OPTION

CONVEYOR BELT

Ursus Maritimus Milking Machine

Leo looked for the sun, found it, calculated where north would be and shook his fist in that direction. 'Fixit International Inc. will not put up with a world where all ice-cream is in the hands of one evil organisation. We will defeat you, IDL.'

Mina looked at her phone. 'After we do our homework. It's getting late.'

Leo scowled, then nodded. He shook his

fist northwards again. 'We will defeat you after we do our homework.'

His phone beeped. He had a message: *I am in ur life gettin ma revenge* ☺ *WW.*

Leo sighed. One day, he'd do something about Wild Wilbur. But right now International Fixit Inc. had more important things to do, like saving ice-cream for the world, and because tomorrow was Saturday, they'd have two whole days to do it.

CHAPTER 13

On Saturday morning, after emptying the garbage, sweeping the front porch and doing a rough sketch of Mrs Giocondo, the next-door neighbour with the strange smile, Leo da Vinci hurried out to the headquarters of Fixit International Inc.

Inside, Isaac the robot was staring at the SlinkyScope. 'My, my,' he said, 'Saturn will be rising early this evening.'

'That's nice,' Leo said, not really listening. He'd had an idea for a drawing with lots of people eating dinner. It'd have to be a long table. 'What is it with you and the stars, Isaac?'

'Astronomy, sir, is like opening the door to the universe.' Isaac opened a small door in his torso and tossed in some wood shavings. Leo thought it looked just like someone eating potato chips – if that someone had their mouth in their chest.

'You've done a lot of stargazing, haven't you?' he asked the robot.

'I have. Your great-great-grandfather let

me use his brass telescope. I study the heavens whenever I get a chance.'

Leo found a pencil but it was blunt. 'Why? The stars don't change.'

'Oh, but the heavens do, especially these days.' Isaac pointed at the screen. 'Satellites, shuttles, the International Space Station – they all move about, disappear and are renewed. And then there are meteors, asteroids and comets – like this one.' He tapped the metal screen with his metal finger. It rang and rippled.

'That's a new comet?' Leo asked.

Ragnar trotted in. 'It's the Big-Kahuna.'

Leo stared at him. 'Sorry?'

'Comet Big-Kahuna,' Ragnar repeated. 'Comets are named after their discoverers, and this one was spotted separately by two astronomers at exactly the same time – Dr Adeline Big and Professor Maisie Kahuna. Comet Big-Kahuna.'

'And is it big?' Leo asked.

Isaac flung his arms wide. His right arm flew off and got tangled in an OctoKittyHiLo doll that was dangling from one of the rafters. Leo reminded himself to tighten the bolts in Isaac's shoulders later.

'It's at least a kilometre in diameter,' Isaac said as he untangled his arm from the doll.

Ragnar nodded. 'It's a whopper, all right.'

A nasty feeling was uncurling in Leo's stomach. 'It's not going to smash into Earth and extinctify us, like what happened to the dinosaurs, is it?'

Leo had spent a lot of time thinking about dinosaurs. He'd decided that they hadn't looked up all that often. He couldn't imagine that they went around like Isaac, for instance, peering at the stars. Everything a dinosaur wanted was at ground level, such as a nice bit of prehistoric grass or a nice bit of dinosaur eating a bit of grass. Things like that.

So Leo decided that they probably hadn't noticed the dinosaur-dooming comet when it appeared as a little sparkle in the night sky. And they probably hadn't noticed it slowly, slowly getting bigger and bigger. And when it finally smashed into Earth, ruining all those nice dinosaur dinners, they were probably like, 'Whoa! Where did *that* come from?'

Isaac laughed, which was like having a cheese grater, a pair of tongs and a cupful of rusty nails all put in a bag and shaken around. 'No, this comet won't do any planet-smashing. Its course is taking it well away from Earth.' He studied the SlinkyScope. 'That's interesting.'

'Interesting in what way?' Leo asked uneasily.

Isaac didn't answer.

Ragnar peered over the robot's shoulder. 'Comet Big-Kahuna has changed course.'

'And that's interesting?'

'Comets don't change course, not unless they stray close to something big,' Ragnar explained. 'And there's nothing big out where it is.'

Isaac straightened. 'That makes two very interesting things about this comet.'

Leo's unease was ramping up. Any minute now he was sure he was going to be in

'I've got a bad feeling about this' territory. 'What's the other thing?'

'Well, its composition is unlike anything ever detected before. All the astronomers are going gaga over it.'

'Going gaga.' Leo tapped his chin with a finger. 'That's a scientific thing, is it?'

'They love a mystery, and this comet is very mysterious.' Isaac opened his firebox and threw in another handful of woodchips. 'You know that comets are made mostly of rock and ice, much like a dirty snowball?'

'Everyone knows that,' Leo said.

'This one seems to be mostly organic matter with hard bits included.'

'Organic matter,' Leo said slowly. 'It wouldn't have the same sort of make-up as ice-cream, would it?'

Isaac clapped his hands together. 'I say, young sir, the figures indicate that it's exactly like ice-cream! Well done!'

Leo winced, his ears ringing. 'An ice-cream comet that's changed its course,' he said, thinking hard. 'Look, you two, I'm going to write something down on this bit of paper while you calculate the new course of this Big-Kahuna.'

'I'm onto it,' Ragnar said. He scurried off, snorting happily.

Isaac studied the SlinkyScope and fed the co-ordinates to Ragnar. In a couple of minutes, they had an answer. Isaac put a hand on his forehead. 'Oh dear.'

'Trouble?' Leo asked.

'The comet's heading straight for us,' Ragnar said. 'Like, kapow.'

'Can you be a bit more precise?'

Isaac checked the SlinkyScope. 'It's going to crash into the North Pole.'

Leo held up his piece of paper, on which were written two words: *North Pole.*

Isaac caught his jaw just before it hit the floor. 'How did you know?' he mumbled once he'd jammed it back on.

'Let's just say I have an idea what the Ice-cream Domination League's up to.'

CHAPTER
14

Mina got to the headquarters of Fixit International Inc. mid-morning. 'Sorry, Leo,' she said, panting, 'I had to mow the lawn.'

'Mow the lawn?' Leo said from one of the workbenches. He was holding up his right arm and trying to sketch how the muscles moved when he clicked his fingers. 'I think I could do something about that.'

Ragnar trotted over. 'No time for lawn-mowing inventions,' he said. 'We've got an ice-cream comet to deal with.'

Mina stared at him. 'What the what?'

Leo explained about the Big-Kahuna. Along the way, he shared his thinking about dinosaurs not looking up.

Mina was impressed. 'So even the ones with the extra-long necks didn't look up? Interesting!'

Ragnar did a little angry dance. 'Guys! This could be the end of the world and you're getting all mooshed up in dinosaur land?'

'You're right, Ragnar,' Leo said. 'Isaac! What's the latest on that comet?'

Isaac was at the SlinkyScope, scratching

his chrome-plated head. A nut came loose and fell to the floor, but Isaac didn't even notice. 'One moment.'

Mina went off to find some better nuts and bolts for Isaac's joints. Leo tried to help Isaac and Ragnar with their calculations, but soon left them arguing about orbits and velocities.

He cleared a space on a bench and spread out a piece of paper the size of a dinner table. He pinned it down, then jumped up on the bench and drew a perfect oval that took up nearly the whole sheet of paper.

He wrote a heading: *TOP-SECRET FIXIT INTERNATIONAL INC. ANTARCTIC BRANCH.* Then he wrote the same heading underneath the first but used his other hand and wrote it backwards. He liked to practise his mirror writing, just for fun.

Leo had been working furiously on the plans for an hour when a knock came at the door. 'Pizza delivery!'

Leo looked up. 'Ragnar, did you order pizza?'

The pig shook his head. 'Nope. Great idea, though.'

Leo opened the door.

'Sanjit's Pizzas,' the scrawny deliveryman said, holding out a box.

'We didn't order a pizza,' Leo replied. Alarm bells were ringing inside his head. Most of them had Wild Wilbur's name on them.

The scrawny guy shrugged and shoved the box at Leo. 'Leave the front light on next time, okay?' he said over his shoulder as he left.

'In the middle of the day?' Leo said, but the deliveryman had already walked out the gate.

Leo felt as if he were holding a bomb – a cheesy, home-delivered bomb. Carefully, he put the box on the nearest bench. He wiped his palms on his shirt. They were sweaty and a bit greasy from the box. He didn't like this. He didn't like it at all. Of course, it mightn't be Wild Wilbur. He thought of all the enemies that he'd made.

International Fixit Inc. had foiled the plans of dozens of supervillains and each one had sworn revenge. He could forget about some, like the Sloth. It'd take that guy ages to get around to doing anything, even if he worked at his fastest.

Others, such as Lady Langtree and the

LADY LANGTREE

THE SLOTH

COUNTESS OF CHAOS

THE ZONE

LEADER OF THE IDL

THE ULTIMATE SMASHINATOR

EDGE OF DARKNESS

LORNA THE PERILOUS

THE UBER-OVERLORD

Countess of Chaos, were in jail. Some, like the Zone, had disappeared. The Ultimate Smashinator was too busy to do any revenging. Stacking shelves at the local supermarket was a full-time job.

Leo's heart thundered and he had to take a deep breath to stop his hands shaking. He lifted the lid of the pizza box as slowly as the Sloth would on a lazy day.

Steam rose from the pizza, all tomato and herbs and cheese. It was covered with olives. They were arranged neatly to spell out a message: *Leonardo da Vinci, I'll have a pizza you soon! WW.*

Leo took a slice of the pizza and bit into it. If Wild Wilbur was going to continue sending threats, Leo hoped they'd be as tasty as this.

CHAPTER 15

After lunch, Ragnar and Isaac resumed their arguing in front of the SlinkyScope.

'We have a situation on our hands, Fixit Internationals,' Isaac announced. 'The Big-Kahuna is definitely bending our way. That can only mean one thing – it's *definitely* being acted upon by an external force.'

'That's what I've been saying all along.' Ragnar snorted. 'The IDL are doing something to bring this ice-cream comet right into their backyard.'

'If that's their plan, it's a pretty good one,' Mina said.

Leo held up a finger. 'If there's one thing better than a pretty good plan, it's a simply amazing plan.'

'And you've got one?' Ragnar waved a trotter at the sketches and plans that cluttered the headquarters like sand dunes. 'Or are you just going to pick one at random?'

'Oh, I have one, all right, and it's a beauty.' Leo gazed at the ceiling, up past the ropes and wires and cobwebs. 'We're going to kidnap that comet.'

Everyone was silent for a moment. Isaac

puffed smoke. Ragnar wrinkled his snout. Mina wrapped duct tape around a wobbly chair leg.

'How?' she asked.

'Simple,' Leo said. 'We'll zoom out and change its course away from the North Pole.'

'To where?' Ragnar asked.

'To the South Pole.' Leo darted to the front bench, scrabbled around for a while, then held up his sketch. 'This is International Fixit's Antarctic Branch.'

Ragnar stared. Isaac stared. Mina stared, while fixing duct tape to a loose floor tile.

'Nice skating rink,' Ragnar finally said, 'and I like the multistorey bowling alley.'

Isaac wasn't convinced. 'This will be difficult to build,' he pointed out. 'As I

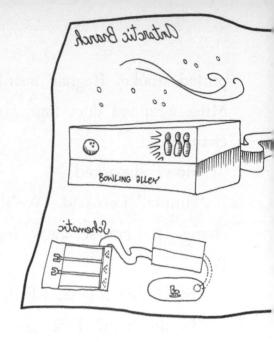

understand it, the South Pole is extremely cold and very, very windy.'

'And that's where you come in, Isaac,' Leo said.

'I do?'

'What's that in your chest?'

'A boiler and a firebox . . . Oh.'

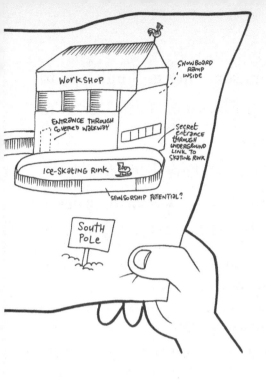

Leo nodded and smiled. 'With your in-built heating, you'll be able to work on the special International Fixit Inc. Antarctic Branch while we're herding the Big-Kahuna your way.'

Isaac straightened his shoulders. He tightened the gasket on one of them and straightened them some more. 'I'm happy to do what I can, but that's a big facility and I'm just one robot.'

Leo marched over and grabbed Isaac by the arms and spoke urgently. 'Isaac, the Mighty Fabricator in Basement Level 3 is making two hundred robots. You'll be in charge of them. You'll be the boss bot.'

'Really? I'll be in charge?'

'You're the robot for the job, Isaac.' Leo noticed then that Mina was looking troubled. 'What's wrong, Mina?'

Mina nodded, then shook her head, then nodded again. 'I've always wanted to go to space,' she said. 'But . . .'

'But what?'

'I'm in charge of Fixit International Inc. repairs, right?'

'You're a vital part of the organisation,' Leo agreed. 'And that's why we need you on this space mission.'

'That's the problem.' Mina held up a roll of duct tape. 'I'm not sure if this stuff works in space.'

CHAPTER 16

The entire International Fixit Inc. team took the fastest lift down to Basement Level 5. As they went past Basement Level 3, Leo had to brace himself against the shuddering and shaking and rattling. The Mighty Fabricator was clearly hard at work making robots.

'There are all sorts of vehicles down here,' Leo said to Mina. The lift doors opened and they all stepped out. 'But this is a job for the Gap-a-tron.'

Ragnar went pale. 'Don't tell me you're going to try the Gap-a-tron after what happened last time!'

'I don't think we have a choice. The Big-Kahuna is six hundred million kilometres away, and we need to be back before school on Monday.'

Mina nodded in agreement. 'Monday is Sport Day.' Then she saw what Leo was looking at. Her face fell. 'You want us to go to space in *that*?'

Leo sighed. It was true that the Gap-a-tron looked like a cross between a tiny tots' wading pool and a two-man tent, but that was because it had started out as a cross between a tiny tots' wading pool and a two-man tent. Leo liked the pink seahorses a lot.

The Gap-a-tron had come a long way from where it started. He'd added a nice tough floor, a special power plant, monitor screens and communication panels, a pair of luminous plastic skulls, a bike rack, an aquarium (with no fish in it yet), an artificial-gravity device and lots of lockers for equipment, but it still looked like a tiny tots' wading pool with a tent stuck on top.

'It's our best chance of defeating the IDL,' Leo said to Mina.

'Uh-huh.' Mina inspected the Gap-a-tron. She wasn't impressed. 'So how's it work?'

Leo didn't want to tell her that the Gap-a-tron was really just an experiment. 'It gets rid

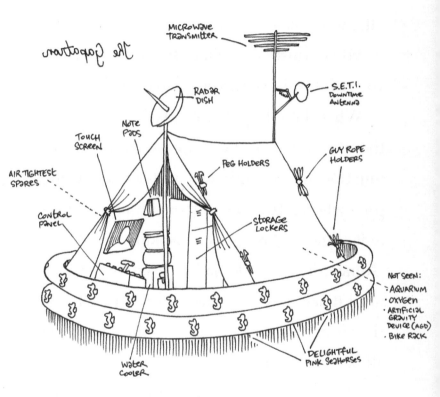

of gaps, so two places that are really far apart are suddenly really close together.'

'Really?'

Leo nodded. 'I've had it jump hundreds of kilometres in a split second.'

Mina whistled. 'Okay, that's snappy, but you still think we can go to space in it?'

What Leo hadn't told Mina was about the times when the Gap-a-tron had malfunctioned. Sometimes, instead of going somewhere, the Gap-a-tron brought things *to* it. Once it brought a crocodile from New Guinea. The reptile hadn't been very happy until it saw Ragnar. Isaac had had to wrestle the croc, tie it up and take it to the zoo. It had all been very stressful.

'Yes,' Leo said, suddenly aware that everyone was waiting for him to answer

Mina's question. 'Yes, I want us to go to space in it.'

'Is it airtight this time?' Ragnar asked. He poked the Gap-a-tron with his snout, and Mina gasped in alarm.

'Of course it is,' Leo said quickly. 'I've sprayed it with AirTightest, one of my latest inventions.'

'And you have plenty of oxygen?' Isaac asked. Everyone stared at him. He shrugged. 'Even though I don't actually breathe, I do understand that it's quite important for you humans. And pigs.'

Leo rolled his eyes. 'The Gap-a-tron is fitted with oxygen tanks, and we'll wear spacesuits when we're outside.'

'And other equipment?' Mina asked.

'Well,' Leo said, 'it's got a bag of tent

pegs, ropes and poles, if that's what you mean.'

'I was thinking about weapons.'

'I've packed it with the sort of stuff that should be useful if we have to go up against the IDL.'

'Fair enough.' Mina gave a little, excited jump. 'When do we leave?'

Leo closed his eyes for a second or two, calculating. 'I have to transport Isaac and his helpers to Antarctica before we head off.'

'What about me?' Mina asked. 'What do I do while you're helping Isaac?'

'Members of Fixit International Inc. show initiative, Probationary Member Mina. While I'm getting Isaac's underlings to the South Pole, find something useful to do. Now, Isaac, to Level 3 and your robot underlings!'

CHAPTER 17

It took more than an hour to transport Isaac and his two hundred robot underlings to Antarctica. When Leo finished, he set the Small Lift to 'Extra Boost' to get to the ground floor fastest.

Even so, he shifted from foot to foot while the floor numbers whirled past. Leo hated to admit it, but he was nervous. The Gap-a-tron had worked perfectly on all fifty trips to Antarctica. That meant it was just getting closer to a glitch. And because it had been so long since the last one, this next glitch could be a biggie.

'Hey, Leo,' Mina said when he stepped out of the lift. 'What do you get when you cross a snowman and a vampire?'

'What?'

'Frostbite!' Mina snorted with laughter and pointed at him.

Leo frowned. 'Are you all right, Probationary Member Mina?'

Ragnar trotted past. 'You've got snow on you.'

'Oh. I see.' Leo brushed the cold white stuff from his shoulders and hair. 'You made a joke, Probationary Member Mina. Very good.'

Mina wiped tears from her eyes. 'You have to have a laugh, right?'

'According to research, it's good for you.' Leo shook the last of the snow from his shoulders. 'Isaac is ready. They've got all the tools they need to start building our Antarctic branch.'

Ragnar squinted at the SlinkyScope. 'I've sent your phone the best co-ordinates I have for the Big-Kahuna. You should be able to track it down.'

'What about you, Probationary Member Mina?' Leo asked. 'What have you done?'

'I've been checking the weapons,' Mina

reported, 'and I've been researching ice-cream. Did you know the Chinese invented it in 3000 BCE?'

'That's interesting, but I'm not sure it helps us with our mission.'

Mina shrugged. 'Just thought it was a fun fact.'

'Maybe, but there's no time for that now. Ragnar, take up your station at the SlinkyScope. Mina, to the Gap-a-tron!'

$$\div$$

Down on Basement Level 5, Leo unzipped the opening of the Gap-a-tron and jumped inside.

Mina quickly followed. 'Hey, nice spacesuits!'

'Thanks. They started off as leopard-print onesies. I made some improvements, especially in the helmet department.'

Mina nodded approvingly. 'Very cool!'

'Suit up, just in case,' Leo instructed.

'Do I have to hang on?' Mina asked when they were all set.

'Not really –' Leo punched the great big green 'go' button – 'because we've reached the comet.'

'What?'

Leo unzipped the door. Outside the Gap-a-tron was the blackness of space. 'If Ragnar has done his sums right,' he said, 'we're floating somewhere outside the orbit of Jupiter.'

CHAPTER
18

'I don't believe it,' Mina said.

'Get ready to believe it, Probationary Member Mina. Jupiter is right outside.' Leo poked his head outside. Off to his right was a bright, stripey disk about the size of a Jupiter-sized coin. 'Oh, there it is.'

'If we're in space,' Mina said, 'how come we're not floating?'

'It's the artificial-gravity device I made.' Leo shrugged. 'Come and have a look outside.'

Mina crawled over and joined Leo. She was quiet for a long time as she looked at the huge universe stretching out in front of them. Finally, she nodded. 'That star is really bright.'

'That's the sun. It's a long way away, but don't look directly at it.'

'How far?'

'If you took a piece of string and stretched it from here to the sun . . .' Leo thought about it for a moment. 'Well, the end would burn up.'

'That far, eh? Amazing.' Mina sat back down. 'Where's the Big-Kahuna?' she asked.

Leo had been wondering the same thing.

'We used Ragnar's co-ordinates, so it should be here somewhere.'

He stuck his head out. He looked right. Nothing. He looked left. Nothing. He looked up. Nothing. He hung his head over the edge and looked down.

Something.

Only a short stone's throw away was a great big blob of a round thing. It was glowing and had a long, sparkling tail that reached out into the void of space. 'Got it.'

Soon, two heads were hanging over the edge of the Gap-a-tron.

'Wow,' Mina said. 'Extra wow, in fact, with a side helping of "whoa".'

'What do you think?'

'Vanilla, I'd say. Maybe with some choc chips.'

Isaac and Ragnar had estimated that the Big-Kahuna was about a kilometre in diameter, which was a lot of ice-cream. About 1,670,000,000,000 kilograms, if Ragnar's rough calculations were correct. *Lots* of ice-cream.

No wonder the IDL wanted to get their hands on it, Leo thought. He vowed then and there that he wouldn't let that happen, not if Fixit International Inc. had anything to do with it.

'Right,' he said. 'Now we just need to find out how the Ice-cream Domination League is steering this thing to the North Pole.'

'I think I know how they're doing it.' Mina pointed up and to the right. 'Watch.'

Leo bumbled around until he could see that a large rocky shape was tumbling towards them. It grew larger and larger and then it zoomed past the Gap-a-tron. It ploughed into the Big-Kahuna, sending up a cloud of ice-cream vapour. The whole comet shook.

'I see,' Leo said. 'The IDL is smashing rocks against the Big-Kahuna to make it change course.'

'Something must be sending the rocks, though,' Mina added.

'Good thinking, Probationary Member Mina.'

'We're a top-class team, Leo. The IDL had better watch out.'

Leo had seen fist bumps before, so he recognised it when Mina held up her curled glove. He'd just never done one before.

'Right,' he said, and gently tapped fists

with Mina. He was surprised at how good it felt. 'I'll contact headquarters.'

He found his phone and opened his Ultra-SuperWave app. 'Ragnar, there's something out here that's sending big chunks of rock at the Big-Kahuna. Is it showing on the Slinky-Scope? It is? Send me the co-ordinates.'

Leo studied his phone. Then he crawled over and punched the figures that Ragnar had sent him into the control panel.

Mina whooped. 'Look at that!'

Leo crawled on his hands and knees and joined Mina at the gap in the tent. Jupiter filled up most of the sky. It looked like someone had thrown a dozen paint pots at it and then spun it really, really fast to make the colours smear right around its surface.

Leo spotted moons, too. Jupiter had

dozens of them, the way a dog had fleas – big, small and in between, with lots of rocks and dust hanging around as well.

It was stunning, but it was a site with plenty of places to hide. 'Where do we even start?' he muttered.

'How about that giant leg over there?' Mina suggested. 'The one made out of ice.'

CHAPTER 19

Hanging in space was the biggest leg made out of ice Leo had ever seen. Quickly, he crawled over to the screen. He punched in the co-ordinates and then whistled. It made his helmet fog up, but he hardly cared. That leg was more than two kilometres long, from the tip of its big toe to the top of its thigh.

Leo crawled back to the gap in the tent. The leg was blue-white and shiny like an iceberg. It had a thigh, a knee, a shin, an ankle and a foot. It floated right next to a long line of round chunks of ice. If the leg was a normal leg, Leo guessed that the chunks of ice would have been about the size of a melon – which would make them nearly a hundred metres across.

The Great Ice Leg started moving. It drifted along until it was just behind the closest of the ice rocks. Leo and Mina watched as it slowly bent at the knee. The foot moved back, back, back until, suddenly, the Great Ice Leg snapped forward. The foot crashed into the ice rock and sent it shooting through space.

Leo counted. The ice rock streaked across empty space until he reached twenty-one. A few million kilometres away, it collided perfectly with the Big-Kahuna.

'It must have been travelling at around 350,000,000 kilometres an hour,' Leo marvelled. 'That Great Ice Leg must be using some sort of space–time enhancer to distort local gravity and impart such momentum.'

'I thought it was taking a penalty kick,' Mina said.

The Great Ice Leg drifted to the next ball of ice. It hung there for some time before it kicked another scorcher right at the comet.

'Someone must be controlling it.' Leo crawled over to a locker. He pulled out a stuffed parrot, a packet of straws and a pair of binoculars. 'Bingo!'

He put the binoculars to his helmet.

'I thought so,' he said. 'Right on top of the thigh is a control room.'

From this distance, the control room looked like a big blister. With his binoculars, Leo thought he could just make out figures moving inside.

Mina punched him on the shoulder. 'Let's go and get 'em.'

While Mina searched for weapons in the Gap-a-tron's lockers, Leo went to the control panel. He sized up the distance and direction of the Great Ice Leg. He punched in some numbers and smacked his fist into his palm.

'Hey, Leo!' Mina held up a blunt metal device. 'What's this?' she asked.

'It's a Recoilless Marshmallow Cannon.'

'It fires marshmallows?'

'The biggest you've ever seen.'

Mina lifted a bunch of other weapons out of the locker. 'And these?'

'That one's a Chopped Nut Gun. That one's a Sprinkles Gun. That one delivers a high-powered stream of chocolate syrup.'

'You've come fully equipped for an ice-cream confrontation, haven't you?'

Leo shrugged. 'Ice-cream and any other freezer-based dessert. Now, here we go.'

Leo hit the big green button.

The Gap-a-tron jolted, and the duo instantly found that they were surrounded by dozens of frogs. The frogs were small, green and spotty. A few started jumping. A few started croaking. Some started jumping and croaking.

'Hmmm.' Leo frowned. 'That didn't quite go as planned.'

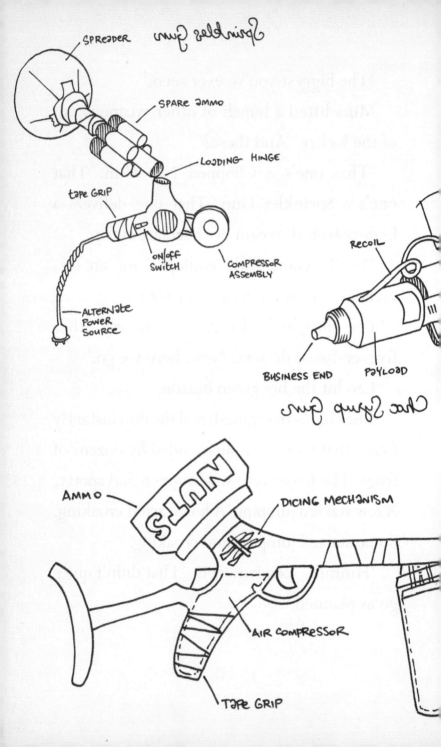

Sprinkles Gun

SPREADER

SPARE AMMO

LOADING HINGE

tape GRIP

on/off switch

COMPRESSOR ASSEMBLY

ALTERNATE POWER SOURCE

RECOIL

BUSINESS END

PAYLOAD

The Syrup Gun

AMMO

NUTS

DICING MECHANISM

AIR COMPRESSOR

tape GRIP

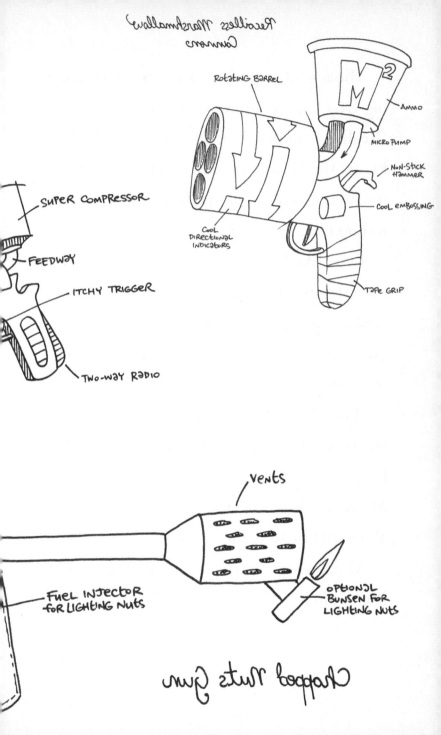

Reveilles Marshmallow Cannon

Rotating Barrel

M²

Ammo

Micro Pump

Non-Stick Hammer

Cool Embossing

Cool Directional Indicators

Tape Grip

Super Compressor

Feedway

Itchy Trigger

Two-way Radio

Vents

Fuel Injector for Lighting Nuts

Optional Bunsen for Lighting Nuts

Chopped Nuts Gun

Mina gently pushed away a particularly big frog that had jumped onto her shoulder. 'Really? I thought they'd come to help. You know, the Deadly Frog Brigade, eager to leap into action and battle the IDL. They're ready to hop to it, I'd say.'

Leo liked the way that Mina always saw the positive side of a situation. Even when she made a mistake, Mina didn't go on about it. She'd make a joke and just move on.

'Frog Brigade. That's good.' Leo turned to the control panel. He had to push a few frogs aside, but he did it gently. 'Probationary Member Mina, the Gap-a-tron is acting up. We might be in trouble.'

Mina peered around suspiciously. 'How bad could it be?'

'I could punch the big green button and a lump of the sun might appear right here.'

'Ouch. Burny.'

'Very, very burny.'

Mina considered this. 'Did you pack any oven gloves?'

'No.'

'Tongs, maybe?'

'No tongs.'

'You'll just have to do it right, then.'

CHAPTER 20

Mina's words inspired Leo. He looked through the binoculars again. He checked the figures that Ragnar had sent. He punched some new co-ordinates into the control panel.

'Fingers crossed,' he said to Mina.

'I would, but it's really hard with these spacesuit gloves.'

Leo punched the big green button.

After a small jolt Mina looked around. 'The frogs are still here.'

'And nothing else has joined them, so that's good.'

Mina peeked out of the tent. 'And we're floating just above the top of the Great Ice Leg. Perfect.'

Leo sighed with relief. It fogged up his helmet. He stuck the Chopped Nut Gun and the Chocolate Syrup Sprayer to his spacesuit with super heavy-duty velcro. 'Ready.'

Mina held up the Recoilless Marshmallow Cannon. 'Ready.'

Leo went first. With Mina right behind him, he pushed himself out of the Gap-a-tron and in the direction of the Great Ice Leg, just as it launched another huge kick at an ice rock.

They drifted towards the control dome. As they got closer, Leo could see three purple-clad figures inside, hunched over controls and screens. Just like the dinosaurs, none of them were looking up.

Mina pointed. Leo nodded. He'd spotted the entrance hatch, too.

They landed. The icy surface was slippery, but they managed to crawl and slide over to the entrance hatch while the Great Ice Leg shook and rumbled with every kick. Leo made a fist and thumped on the hatch one, two, three times.

He put his helmet to the door. A voice came from the other side. 'Who's there?'

'Liniment delivery for the Great Ice Leg!'

'Oh, just what we need! Wait a second.'

The door clunked and groaned, then it swung inward. Leo and Mina stepped into an airlock – a bare, tiny room with another door. Leo pushed the outer door closed and waited while the pressure equalised.

The second door swung inward. Mina was ready. She threw herself in, firing her Recoilless Marshmallow Cannon. Dozens of soft, sticky globs thumped into the purple IDL technician.

'Aaaaaaaargh!' the technician cried as she was hurled backwards. 'Are these marsh-mallows sugar-free?'

The control room was oval-shaped, maybe twenty metres long and about half that wide. The dome overhead was probably five or six metres at its tallest. The place was packed with panels of blinking lights, screens, buttons, levers, dials and other stuff that made it look really busy and important.

Two purple-clad figures were turning away from the control panels. One was a minion. The other was the Leader of the IDL. 'You!' she snarled.

'V!' Mina chirped. 'I love alphabet games!'

Leo didn't quite get the joke, but he didn't wait for Mina to explain it. He ripped the Chocolate Syrup Sprayer from the velcro and blasted away.

'Noooooooooo!' the minion yelled, but it soon turned into, 'Yummmmmm!', as he slid to the far end of the control room.

The Leader of the IDL was quicker or smarter or both. She threw something at Leo and Mina, who'd been foolish enough to stand close together. The table-sized panel tumbled as it flew in the reduced gravity. It smacked them both off their feet before it shattered into a thousand pieces.

Mina struggled to her feet and brushed crumbs off her helmet. 'We've been wafered! Let me at 'em!'

'Too late,' Leo groaned.

The Leader of the IDL had dragged her comrades to a port and pushed them inside. A moment later an escape pod blasted off.

Leo kicked the wafer crumbs aside. 'Well, at least we stopped their Great Ice Leg.'

'And we're totally safe,' Mina said. 'I mean, unless they hit that "self-destruct" button over there before they ran away.'

'Oh, they wouldn't have done that,' Leo said.

'Uh-huh. So that clock isn't really counting down,' Mina said. She pointed at the big red digits on the wall.

'On the other hand,' Leo said, 'maybe we should get a good distance away.'

'Yeah,' Mina said, yawning. 'I suppose we should hurry. If we can be bothered, that is.'

'What?' Leo said, puzzled. Then he realised what was going on. They were in a 'play it cool' contest! How exciting! He'd seen these at school, when two or more kids tried to outdo each other in being laid-back, but he'd never been included in one before. And now, out here in space, it was his chance. He rubbed the back of his head. 'Well, you know, this thing is going to blow up sometime soon, so getting out is a good idea.'

Mina shrugged. 'If you think so.'

'Hey, I didn't mean to get you nervous or anything. Relax.'

'Whoa, I'm so relaxed that I'm almost asleep. How long have we got?'

'Hmm?' Leo said. 'Sorry, I just drifted off for a while. What's your problem?'

'Problem? I've got no problems except staying awake. But don't let me stop you running out of here like a scaredy baby.'

'Thanks, but I'm comfy.' Leo raised his arms and stretched. 'After you.'

'No, Leo, after you.'

Leo glanced at the clock on the wall. Then he looked again. Cool and brave was good, but cool and blown up was very, very bad. 'I'm getting out of here!'

'Not before I do!'

They both threw themselves at the airlock.

CHAPTER 21

Leo arrived back at the Gap-a-tron first and started punching co-ordinates into the control panel. Mina was inside a second later and pushing frogs out of her way. A jolt and they were on the other side of the Big-Kahuna.

'Why are we here?' Mina asked. 'Why didn't we just go home?'

'We need to re-route this comet,' Leo said.

He'd decided to settle the Gap-a-tron on the Big-Kahuna, then use the Gap-a-tron's power to whisk the ice-cream comet to the South Pole, where Isaac and his crew were making ready. It was an easy plan, one that couldn't go wrong as long as the Gap-a-tron worked properly.

Leo turned to find that Mina was on her back, under one of the control panels with interested frogs perched all over her. 'What are you doing, Probationary Member Mina?' he asked.

'Just seeing if there's anything I can fix.'

'And?'

'I taped up a few loose wires.'

'That's all?'

'Well, since I had a hammer, I felt bad about not using it.'

'So you hammered a few things.'

'Not hard or anything. They were more like light taps.'

'I'm not sure that a few light hammer taps are a good idea in a machine that works on quantum nuclear astrodynamics.'

'Don't worry, Leo, you do good work. It'll be fine.'

Leo's brow wrinkled and he rubbed his hands. He'd just had a great idea. Maybe he should give up trying to catch Mrs Giocondo's quirky smile with oil paint. Maybe the best way would be to use crayon –

'Leo.' Mina was nudging him in the ribs. 'What are you doing?'

'Sorry, just got distracted.'

'I notice you do that.'

'It's a problem?'

'Hey, daydreaming's fun, especially when it helps you invent the coolness you come up with.'

Leo felt good about that, and turned back to the controls. Eventually, they edged the Gap-a-tron closer to the Big-Kahuna in the good old-fashioned way. Mina jumped out with a rope, anchored it and the two of them hauled away.

Together, they made the Gap-a-tron nice and solid on the ice-cream surface of the comet. Leo used the ropes and tent pegs. Mina dug up some big choc chips and stowed them inside to weigh down the machine.

When they were done, Leo stood back

with his hands on his hips. He inspected the Gap-a-tron. He looked around at the softly glowing ice-cream comet. 'I think we're ready,' he announced.

Mina stuck out a fist. Leo stared at it, then remembered what he was meant to do. He bumped fists and gave a little wrist twist at the end, just for extra cool.

'Look,' Mina said, 'if this goes really badly wrong and we end up in the middle of a black hole, I want you to remember something.'

'Yes?'

'That I really didn't want to end up in the middle of a black hole.'

Leo nodded. 'That makes sense.'

'One more thing – I've had the best fun ever.'

Leo thought of many things he could say.

None of them seemed right, even if they were true. Instead he said, 'Me too,' and when Mina grinned, he knew he'd made the best choice.

They climbed inside the Gap-a-tron. The frogs were clustered around the choc chips that Mina had shoved inside. For a second they looked guilty, then went back to licking the chocolate with their long, sticky tongues.

Leo put out a finger to push the big green button and then paused and drew back. 'Mina? You want a go?'

Mina grinned. 'Why not?'

CHAPTER 22

One minute they'd been surrounded by the black of space, the next it was white all around.

The Gap-a-tron was rocked by a fierce wind. When Leo unzipped the tent opening, a flurry of white stuff blew in. He took off his helmet. 'It's just snow.'

'Not ice-cream?' Mina asked.

'I don't think so. We must be in Antarctica. Now we have one tiny problem.'

'I'm glad it's a tiny problem. I'm getting sick of those great, big monster-truck sized problems.'

'We're sitting on top of a ball of ice-cream a kilometre in diameter, which means that we're a thousand metres above the surface of the South Pole,' Leo said. 'Even if we tie all our rope together we'd be –' Leo put both forefingers on his temples and did some calculating – 'a long way from the ground.'

'Time for the Gap-a-tron?'

'Let's disconnect it from all this ice-cream.'

Mina frowned. 'What are we going to do with all these frogs?'

Leo had grown so used to having the frogs

around he'd forgotten about them. Snow and frogs weren't a good mix, though. 'Herd them up and put them in the aquarium,' he said. 'Use a bit of cardboard to keep them in.'

One by one, Mina hunted down the frogs and put them in the old aquarium. Then she heaved the choc chips outside. Leo went out and pulled up the tent pegs that were holding the Gap-a-tron down. His spacesuit kept out the cold, but he had trouble holding his feet because the wind was so strong.

Finally, he finished and crawled back inside. 'Let's get to the surface,' he gasped.

'Make it quick,' Mina said. 'The frogs are angry because we threw out their chocolate. I think they're planning to push off the cardboard and mug us.'

'Don't worry about them. Let's go and see

how Isaac and his underlings have been doing.'
Leo punched the big green button.

When they jumped out of the Gap-a-tron, they found themselves in the middle of a ring of hundreds of figures covered in snow. It was like being greeted by a bunch of snowmen.

'A welcoming committee,' Mina said after she took off her helmet. Her teeth started chattering. 'Amazing!'

Together, the snowy figures shook and the snow fell away. Two hundred purple warriors with big ice-cream guns took a step forward. One of them took two steps forward. Her black hair whipped around in the wind and she adjusted her Leader of the Ice-Cream Domination League hat.

'The Big-Kahuna belongs to us,' she snapped, and pointed at the kilometre-high

ball of ice-cream that was looming over them all. 'Back off!'

Leo gazed at the ring of purple warriors. Where were Isaac and his robot helpers? His shoulders slumped. He and Isaac went back a long way.

'That comet is ours,' Mina said. 'Finders keepers.'

'And now *we've* found it, *we'll* keep it.' The Leader of the Ice-cream Domination League shook her gun. 'I'm not happy about the way you destroyed our Great Ice Leg, either.' She stomped her foot. 'I've had enough of you, Leonardo da Vinci! This time your time is up.'

'That doesn't make sense,' Mina pointed out. 'What time is up?'

'You know what I mean.'

'Hey,' Mina said, 'don't go waving that gun around. You could hurt someone. Or make them really, really sticky.'

The Leader of the IDL pulled the trigger. A blob of strawberry ice-cream smacked into Mina's leg.

'Ow!' Mina limped around in a little circle. 'That hurt! Cut it out!'

'Then stay out of this, or the next one will be right in the gut. And, let me tell you, you don't want to be winded by a chunk of pistachio gelato.'

'Leave her alone,' Leo said, stepping forward. 'I'm the one who ruined your plans.'

'Ruined?' The Leader of the IDL laughed. 'You think you were smart, bringing the Big-Kahuna to the South Pole, don't you? Well, now that we've taken over here it just means that we have both the North Pole *and* the South Pole in our hands.'

'They must be big hands,' Mina said. 'And they'd get really cold, this being a polar region and all. So you'd need really big gloves on those really big hands.'

The Leader of the IDL stared at Mina. 'Who *is* this?' she asked Leo.

'This?' Leo put a hand on Mina's shoulder. It was a bit tricky, as Mina was bent over and scraping strawberry ice-cream off her knee. 'This is Mina. She's my friend.'

'What?' Mina straightened. 'Well, of course we're friends.'

'*And* she's second-in-command of International Fixit Inc.'

'Me?' Mina's grin was so bright Leo thought it might cause sunburn. '2IC?'

'You've earned it.'

'So no more "Probationary Member Mina"?'

'Not ever.'

'Do I get a hat? With 2IC on it?'

'Maybe.'

'What about a badge? Or a card, at least — something I could show my mum and dad.'

'We'll see.'

'I don't hate to interrupt this touching scene at all,' the Leader of the IDL said. She smiled a slow, nasty smile. 'Tell me, does this mean I have the top International Fixit Inc. people right here?'

Leo and Mina looked at each other.

'Well, there's Ragnar, but he's not really a people,' Leo said.

'So if the IDL imprisons you here, Fixit International Inc. will be helpless?'

'What?' Leo said. 'You can't do that! We'll miss school!'

'Oh, I forgot.' The Leader of the IDL drummed her fingers on the barrel of her gun. 'Okay, so what about I let you go to school, but then you rush back and I imprison you outside school hours?'

'Sounds reasonable,' Leo said. 'What about sport practice?'

'And on Tuesdays I have to cook dinner,' Mina added.

Leo smacked himself on the forehead. 'Tuesdays! Next Tuesday I start rehearsals for the school play.'

'Are you in the play?' Mina asked Leo.

'I'm a munchkin, but I get to sing and dance.'

'I didn't know you could sing.'

'I didn't either.'

'If you don't mind,' the Leader of the IDL barked. Leo and Mina snapped to attention. 'Just fill out a timetable and give it to one of my minions. We'll work out an imprisonment schedule.'

'You have minions?' Mina asked, impressed.

The Leader of the IDL swept an arm around at the ring of purple warriors. 'I have many, many minions, all dedicated to dominating all ice-cream everywhere!'

'And what do *you* do about school?' Mina asked. 'Just interested, you know.'

'I take correspondence lessons,' the Leader of the IDL replied. 'They're very good. It's amazing what you can learn that way.'

'We should look into that,' Mina said to Leo.

'It's a possibility,' he said, 'but we'd miss out on the social interac—'

Leo was cut short by a loud rumbling. It seemed to be coming from around the feet of the IDL minions.

'Snowquake!' Mina shouted. 'Hit the slush!'

Leo grabbed her arm. 'No – look!'

Two hundred robots burst through the snow, forming a ring around the ring of IDL minions. Black smoke jetted from their chimneys. They stepped forward and wrapped the minions up in their steel arms.

One robot didn't stop there. It marched into the centre of the ring and tapped the Leader of the IDL on the shoulder. 'May I have your weapon, please?' it said.

'Isaac!' Leo shouted. 'You're okay!'

'Okay and extremely cunning, young sir,' Isaac said. He tossed the ice-cream gun to Mina. 'Ragnar sent us a message that the IDL was on its way here, so we buried ourselves, held our smoke and waited.'

'Good plan,' Mina said. She accidentally

hit a button on the gun and a jet of caramel spurted out. 'Whoops.'

'So,' the Leader of the IDL said, 'what happens now?'

CHAPTER 23

Mina climbed out of the Gap-a-tron and stretched. 'You know, Leo, that was the best fun.'

'I'd never really thought of it like that,' Leo said. 'Saving the world *is* the best fun.'

'Blowing up that Giant Ice Leg – I mean, wow.'

'Wow,' Leo echoed. 'That's a good word. I think I'll start using it.'

Isaac nearly tripped as he got out of the Gap-a-tron. 'Those frogs will need a better home,' he said, 'and they're complaining about the lack of chocolate.'

'You understand frog language?' Mina asked.

'It's simple if you listen hard enough.'

'You'll have to teach me sometime.'

'I'd love to.'

They took the Small Lift up to the ground floor. When they stepped out, they were nearly knocked over by one very happy pig.

'You did it!' Ragnar squealed. He ran around them in a little circle, snorting happily.

'I never thought you guys would manage without me but you proved me wrong.'

Isaac bowed, his waist letting out a rusty screech. 'It wasn't easy without you, Ragnar, but we managed.'

'It was important to have you back at headquarters, though,' Leo added. 'We had to have someone who could swoop in and save us if things went wrong. Someone brave, someone smart, someone who would do the right thing in an emergency.'

'Someone porky,' Mina added.

Ragnar nodded. 'Sounds like me. In fact, Mina, it sounds so much like me you might need to wear the Obvious Hat for a week.'

All eyes turned to the pink, pointy, glittery

Obvious Hat. Everyone shuddered except Mina.

'I'd been wondering about that hat,' she said. 'I have to put it on now?'

'That's right,' Ragnar said. 'It's punishment for being so obvious.'

Leo marched over to the Obvious Hat. He screwed it up and stuffed it into the hat recycling bin. 'You know what? No more Obvious Hat,' he declared. 'From now on we can all be as obvious as we like.'

'That's a big decision,' Ragnar said.

'International Fixit Inc. doesn't need to embarrass its members. We're all in this together.'

Ragnar nodded. 'I like it.' He gave a happy snort. 'What did you end up doing with the Leader of the IDL?'

'We took her to the supervillain prison,' Leo said. 'She'll have a special program with time out to go to school.'

'Her minions are going to be helping Isaac's robot underlings at the South Pole,' Mina added.

'Actually, that's where I'll need your assistance,' Isaac said to Ragnar. 'We need to work on the most efficient way to get the ice-cream from the Big-Kahuna to the new Vinci Ice-cream Works.'

Ragnar wrinkled his snout. 'Hmm . . . I have an idea, but I'll need to argue with you about it.'

'Excellent!' Isaac said.

Leo and Mina left the robot and the pig arguing away gleefully.

The mission had been exhausting but it

had been successful. Leo was sure he could have done it alone, but it had been much more fun with Mina. Maybe that was why all those people went to all that trouble to have friends.

He felt a twinge in his stomach. He hoped it wouldn't start growling. 'Are you hungry?' he asked Mina.

'Hungry? You bet.'

'We can get something good at Dad's restaurant. He said I could bring a friend whenever I liked.'

Mina held out a fist. Leo gave it a bump-twist-bump.

'Cool,' Mina said. 'Let's eat.'

They left the headquarters of International Fixit Inc. and crossed the yard.

Leo stopped when he spotted a banner that had been draped over the back door. *Welcome home, Leonardo!* it read, and underneath: *Still gonna get you — WW.*

Mina nudged him. 'Come on, we have to do something before your stomach growls kick off an earthquake warning.'

Leo softly smacked his fist into his palm. He *really* must do something about Wild Wilbur.

But it could wait till after dinner.

LEO DA VINCI

WATCH OUT FOR
BOOK TWO
IN JANUARY 2016

MICHAEL PRYOR has published more than twenty-five fantasy books and over forty short stories, from literary fiction to science fiction to slapstick humour. Michael has been shortlisted six times for the Aurealis Awards, has been nominated for a Ditmar award, and six of his books have been Children's Book Council of Australia Notable Books. Michael's most recent books include The Chronicles of Krangor series for young readers, The Laws of Magic series and The Extraordinaires series for older readers, as well as *10 Futures*, a collection of interlinked stories imagining what our next 100 years might be like, and middle-grade technothriller *Machine Wars*. For more information about Michael and his books, visit www.michaelpryor.com.au.

JULES FABER is a multi-award-winning cartoonist and illustrator. He has published numerous comic strips, worked for various newspapers, taught cartooning around Australia, been in multiple art exhibitions and has worked as an animator on a Disney show. And on top of all that, he loves illustrating children's books, including Anh Do's WeirDo series (Scholastic), *Helix and the Arrival* by Damean Posner and the new Leo da Vinci series by Michael Pryor.

12/15